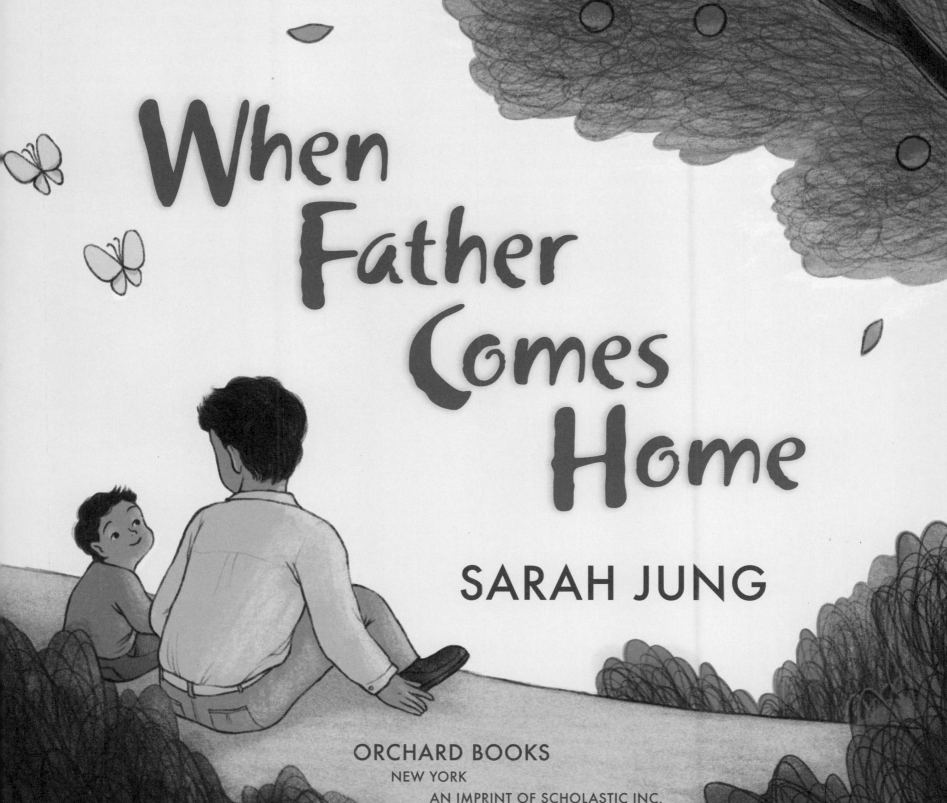

When Father Comes Home

SARAH JUNG

ORCHARD BOOKS
NEW YORK
AN IMPRINT OF SCHOLASTIC INC.

"Will Father come home tomorrow?" June asks as he gets into bed.

"You asked that last night!" says his older brother, Hyun.

"Your father is like a goose," Mother says. "He flies across the world and comes home to us when he has plenty of stories to tell."

Soon enough, June returns from school and sees a big pair of shoes by the door. "Appa!"

"June!" says Father as he sweeps June into a tight hug.

June doesn't see his father very often,
but he is happy when Father is home.
Especially because his mother is happier,
and the food smells more delicious.

When it is bedtime, Father and Mother tuck June and Hyun in. Father tells a story about tigers circling around two brothers, but an angel comes to protect them. June loves to hear this story, and imagines three large tigers roaming out from the wallpaper in their room! But he is not afraid.

June's favorite fruit is a tangerine. "Isn't it both sweet and sour? There are two flavors in one fruit," Father always says. June and Hyun see who can peel their tangerines most creatively. Hyun makes a star, and June makes an elephant. "Where did you learn to do that?" Father asks.

Then Father has a great idea. He decides to plant a tangerine tree in their backyard. June and Hyun clear the plants and dirt around the base of the tree, while Mother and Father hold the tree steady. Father tells June, "Next time I am here, this tree will be bigger, and so will you."

After a long day, Father gives June a piggyback ride. He sings to him as well. Father's voice is low and calm. June can hear Father's feet slide along the wooden floors. When they pass a mirror in the middle of the room, June and Father look at each other and smile.

The day for Father to leave comes too fast.
It is a goodbye that happens often, but every
time it is awkward and sad. June promises Father
to listen to his mother and work hard on his studies.
With long hugs and a kiss, Father leaves.

Without Father home, the house is more quiet. It seems that his absence is a little larger than before.

Every day, June waters the tangerine tree.

"If you grow and I grow, Father will be here sooner. Grow, little tree!" June whispers.

One night, June sees his mother crying in the kitchen. "Don't worry, June," she says. "They are only small tigers." June doesn't understand what she means, but he gives her a tight hug. June doesn't like to see his mother cry.

The next day is sunny with a perfect breeze. June, Hyun, and Mother spend the afternoon in their backyard. The brothers skip across the yard, when suddenly . . .

. . . June trips and falls on the tangerine tree. He begins to cry. "Now Father will never come home!"

Mother sweeps June into a tight hug and wipes away his tears. "Things that have fallen can be replanted. Father has left, but he will always return," she says.

It is not a simple task, but they all get to work. They lift the trunk and pack its roots together. Soon, the tangerine tree is standing again.

Mother smiles at June. "Now it will grow even stronger."

"As long as we hold him tight,
Father will never fly too far!" June says.
It is dinnertime, and June and Hyun help
Mother prepare.

And the food smells delicious.

AUTHOR'S NOTE

When Father Comes Home is based on the Korean phrase 기러기 아빠 (gireogi appa) or "goose dad," a term that describes fathers who work and live apart from their families, flying back to Korea for long periods of time in order to provide for their children's education. These migrant fathers are quietly deemed heroic within immigrant communities for their choice to live one of the most physically and emotionally taxing ways of life, all in the hopes of widening the field of opportunity for their children. Their time spent apart from family comes with consequence—missing out on the growth of their children in their formative years—but it is all in good sacrifice.

June's story is partly inspired by my own. I grew up in Canada with my mother, father, and younger sister, and I can recall memories when my father wasn't there. Each time he came back, he felt more and more foreign to me. But his willingness to bond with me was strong, and the questions that he had for me were constant and the same. My dreams and the things I cared about were just as important to him as they were to me.

While I drew this story from very specific and personal roots, it is really for anyone who has ever struggled with a parent's absence, in whatever form that may take. It can be difficult to ignore the tigers that circle us when we feel afraid. But even in our lowest moments we can find the strength to get back up.

This story is a love letter for my family, written as a tribute to express that after all we've been through, despite all the hardships, and even now when we are separated by waters that divide us, we are still together. We are still here for each other, and love each other, and no country or force of nature could alter that fact.

— Sarah Jung

For Appa

All rights reserved. Published by Orchard Books, an imprint of Scholastic Inc., *Publishers since 1920*. ORCHARD BOOKS and design are registered trademarks of Watts Publishing Group, Ltd., used under license. SCHOLASTIC and associated logos are trademarks and/or registered trademarks of Scholastic Inc.

The publisher does not have any control over and does not assume any responsibility for author or third-party websites or their content.

Library of Congress Cataloging-in-Publication Data available

ISBN 978-1-338-35570-3

10 9 8 7 6 5 4 3 2 1   20 21 22 23 24

Printed in China   38 | First edition, November 2020

The text type was set in Futura T1 Medium. | The display type was set in Khaki Std 1.
The illustrations were created digitally, using Adobe software with graphite medium on velvet fine art paper.

Book design by Marijka Kostiw